Here I am at my first Communion

This book belongs to

_____

A gift for my first Communion on...

_____

At...

_____

From...

_____

A Bible verse for my first Communion

MY FIRST
COMMUNION

Angela M. Burrin

illustrated by Maria Cristina Lo Cascio

Creation

GOD LOOKED AT WHAT HE HAD DONE. ALL OF IT WAS VERY GOOD!

GENESIS 1:31

Receiving Jesus for the first time in Communion is a joyous occasion and one that you will remember for the rest of your life. It marks a very special moment in your friendship with Jesus.

Long before the creation of the world, there was nothing. Nothing but God. God the Father, Jesus the Son and God the Holy Spirit existed before the very beginning of time: a Trinity of love.

But God—Father, Son and Holy Spirit—did not want to keep His love to Himself. He wanted to share it. So God created an amazing world; the heavens and the earth. He created everything that was made in the natural world. And the high point of his creation—the greatest expression of His love—was that He created human beings. He created people to love and cherish: His very own children.

God planned for you to be part of His family. He loves you. He has loved you since before the day you were born. You are His special child.

Welcome to God's family of love.

I'm so happy you are part of our family of love.

THANK YOU, JESUS, FOR MY FIRST COMMUNION.

Adam and Eve

GOD CREATED HUMANS TO BE LIKE HIMSELF...
GOD GAVE THEM HIS BLESSING.
GENESIS 1:27–28

Adam and Eve were the first people in God's family of love. They lived in the beautiful Garden of Eden. Every evening, they walked and talked with God—just the way that Jesus wants to walk and talk with you every day.

God provided wonderful things for Adam and Eve to eat, including fruit, seeds and grains. But there was one tree in the middle of the garden that they couldn't touch. God told them not to eat its fruit. One day, curiosity got the better of Adam and Eve, and they disobeyed what God had asked. First Eve, and then Adam, ate the fruit from the forbidden tree. When they realised what they had done, they were so ashamed that they hid from God.

With great sadness, God sent Adam and Eve out of the garden. Now they had to fend for themselves. They had cut themselves off from God's family of love.

But God made a promise: He would send His only Son into the world. Only Jesus could bring God's children back into the family of love.

THANK YOU, JESUS, THAT I CAN WALK AND TALK WITH YOU EVERY HOUR OF EVERY DAY.

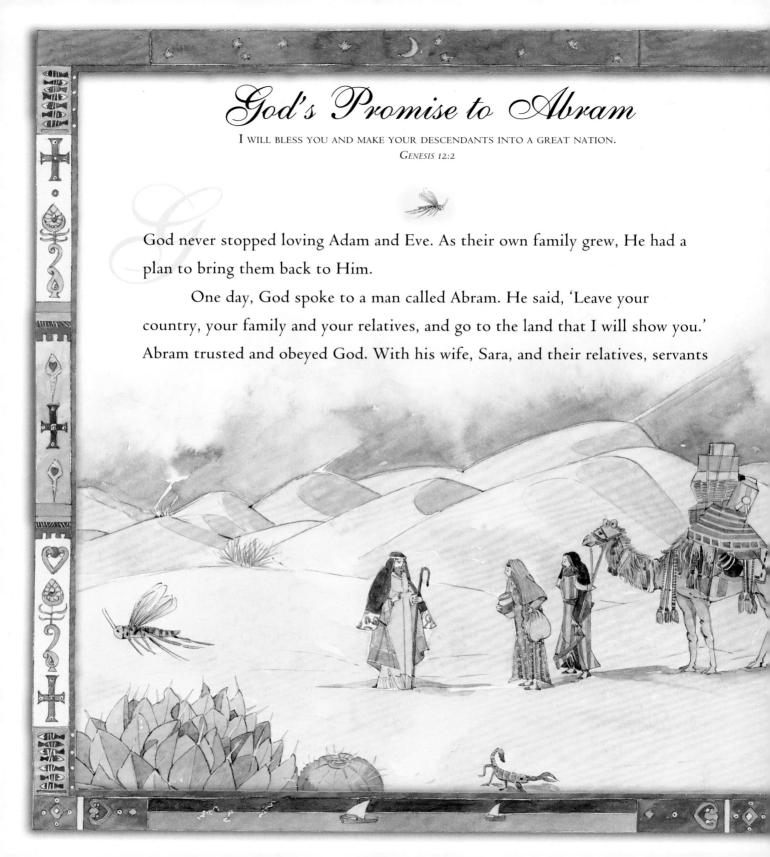

God's Promise to Abram

I WILL BLESS YOU AND MAKE YOUR DESCENDANTS INTO A GREAT NATION.
GENESIS 12:2

God never stopped loving Adam and Eve. As their own family grew, He had a plan to bring them back to Him.

One day, God spoke to a man called Abram. He said, 'Leave your country, your family and your relatives, and go to the land that I will show you.' Abram trusted and obeyed God. With his wife, Sara, and their relatives, servants and animals, they began a long journey. Eventually, they arrived in the country of Canaan. God told Abram that he would be the father of God's special family. Abram's children would be as many as the stars in the sky. God gave Abram the new name of Abraham, which means 'Father of many nations'.

Everyone who belongs to God's family also belongs to the family of Abraham—when Jesus was born, he was one of Abraham's descendants! God's children have Jesus as a brother! You can trust Jesus in the way that you would trust your closest family member. You can tell him anything. He will bless those you love. He will always listen to you.

THANK YOU, JESUS, THAT YOU ARE MY BROTHER. I TRUST YOU.

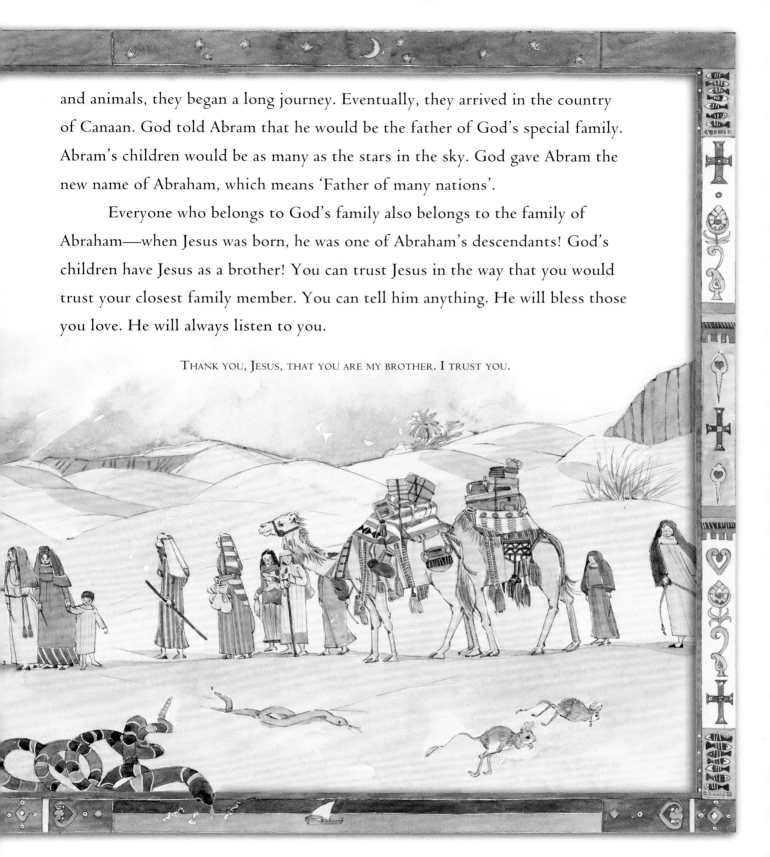

The Passover

God's special family had many adventures. They became known as the Israelites. They lived in Egypt, and Moses was their leader.

The Israelites were the slaves of Pharaoh, the ruler of Egypt. But God wanted to free them. He asked Moses to go to Pharaoh and say, 'Let my people go!' When Pharaoh refused, terrible disasters fell on Egypt. Finally, God told Moses that the time had come for the Israelites to leave. He asked them to prepare and eat a meal of roasted lamb, bitter herbs, and unleavened bread. He told them to put the blood of the lamb over the doors of their houses to protect themselves from death. That night, all the firstborn of the Egyptians died. But the Israelites were kept safe.

The Israelites called their last meal in Egypt 'Passover' because death had passed over them. Moses led the people out of Egypt. When they got to the Red Sea, even the waves parted so that they could pass safely through the waters. They had passed from slavery to freedom.

During Communion, when the bread is broken, the phrase is said: 'Jesus, Lamb of God...'. Jesus is God's Passover lamb. Just as the blood of the lamb protected the Israelites, so Jesus' blood—the Communion wine—will protect you.

JESUS, THANK YOU FOR KEEPING ME SAFE IN YOUR CARE.

Food from Heaven

I AM THE BREAD THAT GIVES LIFE!
JOHN 6:48

What kinds of food do you like to eat? What are your very favourite foods?

Food is very important. When people don't have enough to eat, they get tired and weak. That's what happened to the Israelites after they had escaped from Pharaoh.

The journey through the desert back to Canaan was very long. Food was hard to find. Everyone was hungry. Some people complained to Moses, 'When we lived in Egypt, we could at least sit down and eat all the bread and meat we wanted.' God heard them and said to Moses, 'I will send bread down from heaven like rain.'

The next morning, the ground was covered with white flakes! The Israelites called it 'manna', which means 'what is it?'

Every morning, the same thing happened. Everyone gathered as much as they needed for the day. Now they had strength for their journey.

God looked after His family—and He does the same for you. God has given Jesus to be your spiritual food! Every day you can tell Jesus what you most need. Perhaps it's help with your homework, or the strength to be honest, forgiving or kind. Jesus will help you to be a strong Christian.

JESUS, THE HELP I NEED TODAY IS…

17

The Birth of Jesus

YOUR CHILD WILL BE CALLED THE HOLY SON OF GOD.
LUKE 1:35

Do you like Christmas? It is all about Jesus' birth. Jesus is the person who carried out God's promise to bring Adam and Eve's descendants back into God's family of love.

God chose a young girl called Mary to bring about his promise. He sent the angel Gabriel to Mary to ask her to become Jesus' mother. Mary said, 'Let it happen as you have said.' Mary married Joseph and he cared for her and her baby.

Jesus was born in Bethlehem. A kind innkeeper let Mary and Joseph use his stable. After Jesus' birth, Mary laid him on a bed of hay. That night, something wonderful happened. Thousands of angels sang, 'Praise God in heaven!' Shepherds in nearby fields saw and heard the angels. They came to visit the newborn baby. Later, three wise men travelled many miles to visit Jesus, bringing precious gifts.

You, too, can bring precious gifts to Jesus. When you are in church you can bow your head or kneel down and say, 'Jesus, I love you. Thank you for your birth and for making it possible for me to be part of God's family of love.'

JESUS, THE GIFT I WANT TO BRING YOU TODAY IS…

Jesus Feeds Five Thousand

EVERYONE ATE ALL THEY WANTED.
LUKE 9:17

One hot day, lots of people followed Jesus up a hillside. Some had travelled a long way. Jesus welcomed them. He told them about God's love—just as he tells you. He also healed those who were unwell. Jesus' special friends—the disciples—were with him. Just as the sun was setting, they said, 'Where will we get enough food to feed all these people?' Then Andrew said, 'There is a boy here who has five small loaves of barley bread and two fish. But what good is that with all these people?'

Jesus told his friends to make everyone sit down. He took the loaves and the fish and blessed them. The disciples gave them to the crowd. Everyone had enough to eat. The leftovers filled twelve baskets. Jesus fed over five thousand people that day.

What a wonderful miracle! What a memory those people had of Jesus' care for them! But Jesus has given you more than a memory; he has given himself in the bread and wine at Communion. That is the closest that you will be to him until you are with him in heaven.

JESUS, THANK YOU FOR GIVING ME ALL I NEED.

Jesus Blesses Little Children

LET THE CHILDREN COME TO ME!
LUKE 18:16

Jesus loves all children. And that includes you. He thinks about you all the time.

Jesus loved being with children when he lived on earth. One day, some people wanted to bring their children to Jesus for a blessing. But because he was teaching about God's heavenly kingdom, his disciples stopped them. They didn't want people bothering Jesus.

Jesus said, 'Let the children come to me! Don't try to stop them.' How would you have responded to Jesus' welcoming words? Perhaps you would have run to him. Perhaps you would have brought some flowers, picked from the hillside. Perhaps you would have climbed on his back.

Before the children left, Jesus blessed them all. Jesus was their best friend.

Jesus also gives you many blessings. When you eat the bread of Communion and drink the wine, close your eyes and imagine Jesus is there with you. Thank him for some of those blessings: your family; your friends; the beautiful world he created—and lots more!

JESUS, THANK YOU FOR BEING MY FRIEND.
HELP ME TO BE A GOOD FRIEND TO OTHERS.

22

The Last Supper

EAT THIS AS A WAY OF REMEMBERING ME! *LUKE 22:19*

'Dinner's ready!' Those words often make us stop what we are doing! Eating meals together is very special.

The evening before Jesus died on the cross, he ate a Passover meal with his twelve disciples in an upper room in Jerusalem. Together, they remembered and celebrated how Moses had led God's special people out of slavery in Egypt and into Canaan.

During the meal, Jesus took a piece of unleavened bread, blessed it and broke it, saying, 'This is my body, which is given for you.' Then he took a cup of wine and, after thanking God, said, 'This is my blood, which is poured out for many people.' Jesus' last supper was the disciples' first Communion.

At Communion, in memory of Jesus, the priest holds up the bread and wine and repeats Jesus' words. By the power of God's Holy Spirit the bread and wine is made holy: it becomes the body and blood of Jesus. During this time, look, listen and say in your heart, 'Jesus, I believe that you are really present.'

JESUS, THANK YOU FOR GIVING ME SUCH A SPECIAL WAY TO REMEMBER YOU.

Jesus Is Nailed to a Cross

FORGIVE US OUR SINS, AS WE FORGIVE EVERYONE WHO HAS DONE WRONG TO US.

LUKE 11:4

After supper, Jesus took his disciples to a garden called Gethsemane. It was late at night and his disciples fell asleep. But Jesus prayed to his heavenly Father for strength to accept what God wanted him to do.

Suddenly, Roman soldiers carrying torches came and arrested Jesus. Judas, one of Jesus' friends, had told them where he was.

The next day, the soldiers put a crown of thorns on Jesus' head. They made him carry a heavy wooden cross up the hill to a place called Calvary. The soldiers nailed Jesus to the cross and sat down to guard him. After hanging on the cross for six hours, Jesus died.

At Communion you may hear the words, 'Lamb of God, you take away the sins of the world.' When Jesus died on the cross, he opened the way for God's children to be forgiven and brought back into the family of love. When you receive Communion, think about what happened to Jesus. After you have received the bread and the wine, thank Jesus for dying on the cross. And remember, nothing is ever too big to be forgiven.

JESUS, THANK YOU FOR DYING ON THE CROSS FOR ME.

Jesus Is Alive!

I WILL BE WITH YOU ALWAYS.
MATTHEW 28:20

Very early on Sunday morning, the women went to the tomb—and found it empty! Jesus was alive! He had risen from death!

After the resurrection, Jesus met his disciples in many places: at their homes, on a road, and as they fished on the Sea of Galilee. He spent forty happy days with them!

Jesus explained to his disciples that, although he would be leaving them soon, he would always be with them. He asked them to tell everyone about him: about his life, his death and his resurrection. He promised to send God's Holy Spirit to help them.

Jesus went with his disciples to the Mount of Olives. After blessing them, he was taken up into heaven and they could no longer see him. Just like Jesus' disciples on that day, you cannot see Jesus. But he is always with you. When you wake up you can say 'good morning' to Jesus. During the day, whether you are happy or sad, you can say, 'Jesus, you are with me.' Before going to sleep you can hear him tell you that he loves you.

THANK YOU, JESUS, THAT YOU ARE ALWAYS CLOSE TO ME.

The Coming of the Holy Spirit

THE HOLY SPIRIT TOOK CONTROL OF EVERYONE.
ACTS 2:4

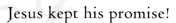

Jesus kept his promise!

After he returned to his Father in heaven, his disciples and other friends went back to the upper room in Jerusalem, locked the doors and prayed. On the tenth day, they heard a noise. It sounded like a strong wind. Then they saw what looked like fiery flames over each other's heads. It was the Holy Spirit!

That day was the day of Pentecost: the beginning of Jesus' Church. It is the Church's birthday!

The Holy Spirit did amazing things in the disciples' hearts. They were no longer afraid. They ran out into the streets and told everyone about Jesus.

Many people wanted to know more, so they joined the disciples. All the people who loved Jesus were like a family to each other. They celebrated Communion and prayed together.

You became part of God's family of love when you were baptised. And now you have received your first Communion!

Jesus' love goes on and on. God's Holy Spirit will help you to keep on loving Jesus.

JESUS, I LOVE YOU. THANK YOU FOR YOUR HOLY SPIRIT!

The Peace

The peace of the Lord be always with you.

God's Love

God loved the people of this world so much
that He gave His only Son,
so that everyone who has faith in Him
will have eternal life
and never really die.

JOHN 3:16

The Lord's Prayer

Our Father, who art in heaven,

hallowed be your name,

your kingdom come,

your will be done,

on earth as it is in heaven.

Give us this day our daily bread,

and forgive us our trespasses,

as we forgive those who trespass against us.

Lead us not into temptation

but deliver us from evil.

Amen

Prayer of Preparation

Almighty God,

to whom all hearts are open,

all desires known,

and from whom no secrets are hidden:

cleanse the thoughts of our hearts

by the inspiration of your Holy Spirit,

that we may perfectly love you,

and worthily magnify your holy name;

through Christ our Lord.

Amen

Prayer after Communion

Almighty God,
we thank you for feeding us
with the body and blood of your Son Jesus Christ.
Through him we offer you our souls and bodies
to be a living sacrifice.
Send us out in the power of your Spirit
to live and work
to your praise and glory.
Amen

The Apostles' Creed

I believe in God, the Father almighty,
creator of heaven and earth,
and in Jesus Christ, His only Son, our Lord,
who was conceived by the Holy Spirit,
born of the Virgin Mary,
suffered under Pontius Pilate,
was crucified, died, and was buried;
he descended into hell;
on the third day he rose again from the dead;
he ascended into heaven,
and is seated at the right hand of God the Father almighty,
from there he will come to judge the living and the dead.

I believe in the Holy Spirit,

the holy catholic Church,

the communion of saints,

the forgiveness of sins,

the resurrection of the body,

and life everlasting.

Amen

A Blessing

The peace of God,

which passes all understanding,

keep your hearts and minds in the knowledge

and love of God,

and of His Son Jesus Christ our Lord;

and the blessing of God almighty,

the Father, the Son, and the Holy Spirit,

be among you and remain with you always.

Amen

God's Protection

God will command his angels to protect you
wherever you go.
They will carry you in their arms,
and you won't hurt your feet on the stones.

The Lord says, 'If you love me and truly know who I am,
I will rescue you and keep you safe.
When you are in trouble, call out to me.
I will answer and be there to protect
and honour you.'

PSALM 91:11–12 AND 14–15

39

Use this page for photographs, Bible verses and prayers
that mark your first Communion.

Use this page to record special memories of your first Communion.

Use this page for photographs, Bible verses and prayers
that mark your journey with Jesus.

*Use this page for photographs, Bible verses and prayers
that mark your journey with Jesus.*

Use this page for photographs, Bible verses and prayers
that mark your journey with Jesus.

Use this page for photographs, Bible verses and prayers
that mark your journey with Jesus.

First edition 2009
Second edition 2025

Scripture quotations taken from the Contemporary English Version of the Bible, published by HarperCollins Publishers, are copyright © 1991, 1992, 1995 American Bible Society.

Extracts from *Common Worship: Services and Prayers for the Church of England* are copyright © The Archbishop's Council 2000 and reproduced by permission.

The Lord's Prayer and The Apostles' Creed as they appear in *Common Prayers* from the *Catechism of the Catholic Church* (Liturgy Office of England & Wales) are copyright © Catholic Bishops' Conference of England and Wales, and are reproduced by permission of the publisher.

Copyright © 2009 Anno Domini Publishing
www.ad-publishing.com
Text copyright © 2009 Angela M. Burrin
Illustrations copyright © 2009 Maria Cristina lo Cascio

Publishing Director: Annette Reynolds
Art Director: Gerald Rogers
Pre-production: GingerPromo, Kev Holt

ISBN 978-1-916546-17-2
Copyright © 2025 Don Bosco Publications
www.salesians.org.uk/bookshop

Printed and bound in China